A Junior Novelization

Adapted by Shannon Penney
Based on the original screenplay
by Amy Wolfram
Illustrations by Ulkutay Design Group
and Allan Choi

SCHOLASTIC INC.

New York   Toronto   London   Auckland

Sydney   Mexico City   New Delhi   Hong Kong

ISBN-13: 978-0-545-09413-9
ISBN-10: 0-545-09413-5

Special thanks to Vicki Jaeger, Monica Okazaki, Tanya Mann, Christine Chang,
Rob Hudnut, Shelley Dvi-Vardhana, Jennifer Twiner McCarron, Pat Link,
Shawn McCorkindale, Walter P. Martishius, Tulin Ulkutay, and Ayse Ulkutay.

Published by Scholastic Inc.
SCHOLASTIC and associated logos are trademarks and/or
registered trademarks of Scholastic Inc.

12 11 10 9 8 7 6 5 4 3 2 1   9 10 11 12 13/0

Designed by Angela Jun
Printed in the U.S.A.
First printing, September 2009

Chapter 1

Long ago, a beautiful girl lived in Gascony, far outside Paris, France. Corinne loved her simple life at the farmhouse with her mother. But part of her had always longed for adventure. Fortunately, she had a good imagination. With it, she created her own adventures!

One afternoon, Corinne was doing just that, fighting an exciting fake duel against a scarecrow in the barn. With a wooden broom handle, she battled with the scarecrow, leaping around the barn with ease.

"You cannot defeat me, for I am a Musketeer!" she cried, lunging at the scarecrow. She knocked the broom out of its motionless hand.

In triumph, she flipped gracefully across the barn and jabbed her broom handle, using it to lift a pail of animal feed.

The feed flew into the air and landed neatly in the nearby troughs. Corinne's chores were done!

Nearby, her spirited kitten, Miette, did her best to imitate Corinne's moves. Miette leaped through the air, flipping wildly. She landed at the hooves of Alexander, the sturdy old barn horse. He couldn't help smiling at the clumsy kitten.

Just then, Corinne grabbed a rope hanging from the hayloft and used it to swing across the barn. Once she was high in the air, she let go, flipped twice — and landed in the hay on her backside. Ouch!

"You need a bit more height if you want to stick that landing," a kind voice called from the doorway.

Corinne looked up to see her smiling mother, Marie. "I'll get it next time!"

Corinne said determinedly, standing and brushing herself off.

Marie's eyes twinkled. "You're determined, just like your father."

"And I'm going to be a Musketeer just like him, too," Corinne said.

"It's a great responsibility to protect the royal family," Marie said slowly, her brow furrowing. "And it can be dangerous."

That didn't stop Corinne. "I've been waiting my whole life for this. We agreed that when I turned seventeen I could go to Paris to —"

"— to be a Musketeer. I know," Marie said, studying her daughter. Then she pulled an envelope from behind her back. "I suppose you'll need this. It's a letter to Monsieur Treville, head of the Musketeers.

He was a friend of your father's. I've asked
him to look out for you."

Corinne's eyes widened as Marie
went on.

"Here are fifteen crowns," she said,
handing Corinne a bag of coins. "You'll
need them in Paris. And I want you to take
Alexander. He knows the way."

The old horse looked up in excitement.

Corinne gave her mother a giant hug. "Thank you!"

"Let's eat, and then off to bed with you," Marie said, leading her daughter back to the farmhouse. "You've got a big day tomorrow."

The next morning, as the sun peeked over the hills, Corinne gave her mother another hug. This time, it was a hug good-bye. Corinne was headed to Paris!

"You must be brave," Marie said, holding tight to her daughter's hands. "Remember what your father taught you: True courage —"

"— is pursuing your dream, even when everyone else says it's impossible," Corinne finished. With that, she climbed easily into Alexander's saddle. "I'll make you proud!"

Marie waved good-bye, her eyes glittering with tears. "You always do," she said.

As Alexander headed into the distance, a furry little blur ran up behind him and leaped into the saddle with Corinne. Miette didn't want to be left behind!

Corinne giggled, patting the kitten's head. "Come, Miette. We're going to Paris!"

Chapter 2

After traveling for many days, Corinne, Alexander, and Miette finally spotted the castle! Alexander galloped onto the streets of Paris.

Corinne took a deep breath, looking around in awe. There was so much to see! The streets were packed with street vendors, shoppers, and playing children. Music rang through the air. Corinne couldn't help being amazed by the beautiful buildings and crowds of people.

Before long, she spotted a boy watching over a group of well-groomed horses. The boy kindly agreed to watch Alexander for a few days. Corinne handed him some coins from her bag, gave Alexander a kind pat, and ran off with Miette at her heels, calling, "I'm going to be a Musketeer!"

The boy shrugged at one of the horses and said, "*She's* going to be a Musketeer?"

Not far down the street, a crowd had gathered. Corinne stood on her tiptoes and was delighted to spot four men in blue tunics, boots, and feathered caps, performing a duel on a set of steps. Their swords clanked as they playfully lashed out at one another. Real Musketeers!

Corinne and Miette could hardly contain their excitement. They watched as the Musketeers battled back and forth, until finally, one swiped the others' swords right out of their hands. The crowd cheered.

"Is anyone brave enough to challenge me?" the winning Musketeer called, peering into the crowd.

This was Corinne's chance! She pushed her way to the front of the group. "I, sir," she said bravely. "I am going to be a Musketeer!"

One of the Musketeers on the steps chuckled. "The little girl wants to be a Musketeer!"

Eager to prove herself, Corinne performed a series of complicated flips. Unfortunately, she landed on a barrel that quickly rolled out from under her. Corinne hit the ground with a heavy thud.

"Why don't you run along and leave the Musketeering to the big boys?" The winning Musketeer chuckled.

Corinne wasn't about to give up. She rose to her feet. "I have a letter for Monsieur Treville. He will make me a Musketeer."

One of the Musketeers pointed across the street with a sneer. "His office is over there." Still laughing, the men went back to dueling as Corinne and Miette crossed the street.

As they approached the gate, a growling French mastiff snatched the letter right out of Corinne's hand! The dog bolted through the marketplace with Corinne and Miette hot on his heels.

He ran past the guards and through the gate to the Musketeer compound. Corinne and Miette followed before anyone could stop them.

With the envelope still in his mouth, the dog trotted into the compound's courtyard, where Monsieur Treville had just finished talking to the royal regent, Philippe. Philippe was the prince's cousin. As regent, it was his job to look after Prince Louis. But now that the prince was about to become king, Philippe's work at the castle was almost done.

Philippe turned to leave and spotted Corinne. "Young lady, are you lost?" he asked.

Corinne stood tall. "I have come to speak with Monsieur Treville about becoming a Musketeer."

Philippe laughed. "As if a girl could ever be a Musketeer!"

"Your dog has my letter," Corinne continued.

Philippe called Brutus the dog over, commanded him to drop the drooly envelope, and left the courtyard with a tip of his hat. Brutus made sure to growl at Miette before following his master.

"Monsieur Treville!" Corinne called to the captain of the Musketeers, a kind-looking man. "I must speak with you!"

Monsieur Treville looked at her, confused. "Do you have a letter of introduction?" he asked.

Corinne held up the wet envelope, looking a bit sheepish. "You knew my father, D'Artagnan."

The captain's eyes lit up. "Why, yes! He was a brave and noble Musketeer. What can I do for you?"

Corinne took a deep breath. "I want to be a Musketeer."

Monsieur Treville couldn't help looking surprised. "But being a Musketeer requires more than just desire. It requires the proper training."

"I have trained every day at the farm," Corinne replied.

"And it requires years of experience," Monsieur Treville went on. "Every Musketeer must first serve his country and perform noble acts."

"I know I can become a Musketeer," Corinne said, looking him in the eye. "Please give me a chance."

Monsieur Treville sighed. "It is a privilege to protect the royal family. I'm sorry, but you're just not ready."

Corinne's face fell.

As Monsieur Treville led her to the gate, he smiled kindly. "If you ever need anything, please come to me."

"Thank you," Corinne replied sadly. She walked out into the street, leaving the compound — and the world of the Musketeers — behind.

Chapter 3

Corinne slumped on the steps outside the compound gate, chin in her hands. Miette rubbed against her leg, trying to comfort her.

Just then, Brutus the dog reappeared. He snarled, and the kitten darted away with the dog right behind.

"Miette!" Corinne called, running after them. "Wait!"

The trio dashed through the streets of

Paris, past stores and through crowds. As they approached a fabric shop, a beautiful young girl about Corinne's age stepped out, wearing a simple maid's outfit and carrying a piece of shimmering fabric. With a quick flip of her wrist, a measuring tape slipped out from under her sleeve. In seconds, she'd transformed the fabric into a beautiful cape.

"*C'est magnifique!*" she exclaimed, pleased with her work.

But at that moment, Miette and Brutus dashed by through a mud puddle, splashing the girl's new cape. Corinne wasn't far behind.

"You're going to pay for this!" the girl cried.

Corinne couldn't slow down, but cried, "Sorry!" over her shoulder.

Up ahead, Miette and Brutus headed
for the city rose garden. Inside, another
young girl in a maid's uniform spun
gracefully among the flowers. When the
kitten ran by, the girl twirled to avoid
her. When the dog followed, the girl
leaped lightly over him. But when Corinne

barreled around the corner, she ran smack
into the girl, sending her flying into a
rosebush!

"Excuse me!" Corinne called,
running on.

"That was rude!" The girl tried to pull

herself out of the rosebush, but her uniform kept snagging on the thorns.

Now Miette and Brutus were quickly approaching the castle. On the bridge, a different girl in a maid's uniform stood playing a beautiful song on the violin. Miette dashed through her legs, with Brutus barreling right behind. The animals startled the girl, and she flung her bow up into the air. It was lost.

As Corinne approached, she wasn't watching where she was going. She slammed right into the maid! The girl tumbled into the moat, catching her precious violin just before it hit the water.

"I'll get you!" she cried after Corinne. She struggled to stand in the moat water. "Just as soon as I get out of here."

Corinne looked back over her shoulder, exasperated and feeling terrible for all the trouble she'd caused. "I'm sorry, but you're going to have to get in line!"

Miette and Brutus continued on, past a set of guards and finally through a little doggy door into the servants' entrance of the castle itself. Corinne stood outside the door, panting. Now what?

Just then, the door was flung open, and a young maid tumbled out.

"You're fired!" a voice called behind her. A strict-looking woman appeared in the doorway.

As the maid hurried away, the woman looked at Corinne. "You'll do." She pulled Corinne inside and slammed the door just as the royal guards appeared around the corner, looking for Corinne. "I am Madame de Bossé. What brings you here?"

Corinne cleared her throat. "I came to be a Musketeer."

An older woman, cleaning nearby, looked up with interest.

Madame de Bossé laughed coldly. "You,

a Musketeer? There are no female Musketeers!"

"Not yet," Corinne said, "but it's my dream."

"Dreams are for sleeping," Madame de Bossé said, waving her hand. "Never mention this nonsense again." She handed Corinne a maid's uniform. "Do you want a job or not?"

The guards who had been chasing Corinne appeared in the doorway, ready to kick her out. Corinne had no choice but to accept the job. "Yes, Madame."

Madame de Bossé led the way into the castle, shouting at the older woman for dusting poorly. "If you weren't the only one who knows where everything is in the castle, I would have fired you long ago, Hélène!"

Aramina looked at the other girls. "I insist she stay with us!" she said with a dramatic flair.

"Got any money?" Renée asked Corinne.

Corinne handed her some coins and grinned gratefully. "Just tell me where you live, and I'll meet you there." She had some unfinished business to attend to.

A little while later, Corinne arrived at the girls' sleeping chambers with Renée's violin bow in hand. She had gone back to the moat to retrieve it. She walked over to Renée's corner of the room. "I thought you might need this."

Maybe Corinne would be friends with these girls after all!

Chapter 4

The next morning, Prince Louis's excited cry echoed through the castle. "And they said it couldn't be done!"

The prince was an eager inventor. At almost eighteen, he was about to take the throne as king, but he was much more interested in gadgets than in ruling. This time, he had discovered how to make a balloon fly through the air on its own!

The little balloon floated down the castle

hallway. Prince Louis followed giddily. Corinne, Viveca, Aramina, and Renée were all polishing the upstairs banister in the grand entrance when the prince ran in. He was busy watching his balloon float up to the ceiling and pop on the chandelier — and he bumped right into Corinne!

"Sorry!" he called, rushing off.

Aramina leaned over to Corinne. "Isn't he the dreamiest?"

Viveca rolled her eyes. "You think every boy is dreamy."

Corinne couldn't help watching the handsome prince as he descended the stairs. Philippe waited for him below.

"Did you see that?" Prince Louis called to the regent. "I developed a prototype balloon! Just think how this will work for my flying machine!"

Philippe sighed. "When will you get it into your head? Man will never be able to fly."

The prince grinned. "Ah, but he will. It's my dream!"

Philippe took Prince Louis by the shoulders and led him to the center of the entryway, directly beneath the chandelier. "We need to plan your birthday celebration."

"You're in charge of the details," the prince said. "My flying machine can't wait!" As he rushed away, the huge chandelier fell with a crash — right where the prince had been standing only seconds before!

Prince Louis was thrown off his feet. The chandelier shattered, sending glass everywhere. But Corinne, Viveca, Aramina, and

Renée instinctively sprang into action to protect the prince. Corinne swiped the flying glass away with her feather duster. Viveca cracked a polishing rag through the air, whipping the glass in the other direction. Aramina spun, giving the debris a graceful and powerful kick. And Renée threw her feather duster into the air, where three pieces of glass hit it all at once and shattered!

After the debris had settled, the girls looked at one another in amazement.

Hélène, the old cleaning woman standing nearby, raised an eyebrow. In all the chaos, she was the only one who had noticed what the girls had done to protect the prince!

The regent's guardsmen rushed into the entryway, pulling Prince Louis to his feet. "Are you all right, Your Highness?" one asked.

Philippe looked around the room. "I demand to know what is going on here!" He turned to one of his men, a tough-looking guy named Bertram. "Make sure this doesn't happen again." Then he ushered Prince Louis out of the room.

Corinne peered at the spot where the rope holding the chandelier had been fastened.

There was a piece of rope on the floor. *If the rope broke, why would there be an extra piece?* Corinne wondered. Had the rope been cut?

Next to the rope, Corinne spotted a shiny red gem glistening in the light. She dropped it into her pocket. Maybe it was a clue!

The girls quickly began cleaning up the broken chandelier.

Renée leaned toward Corinne. "Where did you learn to move like that?" she whispered, so Madame de Bossé wouldn't overhear.

Corinne lowered her voice. "I've been training to be a Musketeer!"

Viveca, Aramina, and Renée all gasped. "Me, too!" they said at once. They looked at one another, shocked.

"Why didn't you say so before?" Viveca asked.

Aramina shrugged. "I thought you would laugh at me. Who would believe in a girl Musketeer?"

"They should allow female Musketeers!" Renée said firmly.

Just then, Hélène appeared behind the girls, grabbing them each by the collars. "Come with me."

Chapter 5

Without a word, Hélène led the four girls through the castle and down a dark tunnel that ended at a bookcase. Corinne looked at her friends, frightened. Where was Hélène taking them?

With a quick push, Hélène flipped the bookcase around.

"A secret passageway!" Corinne said breathlessly.

"I'd heard rumors that the castle had

these, but I've never actually seen one," Aramina added.

Hélène lit a candle, illuminating a set of stairs beyond the bookcase. As the girls entered the secret passage, Hélène tugged on a nearby sconce. The stairs turned into a slide! All four girls whooshed down. At the base of the slide, Hélène somehow appeared in front of them.

"We've arrived," Hélène said, relighting her candle.

Corinne and her friends could see that they'd landed in a grand room, clearly built for training. There were balconies, staircases, ropes, and suits of armor everywhere.

"What is this place?" Corinne asked.

Hélène smiled. "This is the old Musketeers training room." She pulled a tarp off a nearby wall, revealing rows of glistening swords and weapons. "Think you can be Musketeers?" she asked, tossing a sword to Corinne. "Prove it."

Hélène straightened up, grabbed a sword of her own, and engaged Corinne in a duel. Corinne flipped, jumped, and lunged, but Hélène countered her every move. Before long, Corinne's sword went flying through the air. Hélène had won!

Viveca was up next, using a whip she pulled from the weapons wall. She was a skilled fighter, leaping over the whip like a jump rope. But Hélène raised her sword, wrapped the whip around it, and pulled Viveca off her feet.

Aramina jumped into action, tossing two beautiful fans, boomerang-style, across the room to break a board in half. But as one of the fans sailed back to her, Hélène sliced it in half in midair!

"Amateurs," Renée scoffed, grabbing a bow and arrow from the wall. She shot an arrow directly into the center of a bull's-eye across the room, and looked pleased with herself — until Hélène tossed her

sword and cut the arrow right down the middle!

"Teach me to do that!" Corinne cried.

"Me, too!" the other girls added. They had a newfound respect for Hélène.

Over the course of the afternoon, Hélène put the girls through their paces. She taught them proper sword-fighting techniques, urged them to work as a team, and ran them through one exercise after another. After hours of training, the four friends were exhausted.

"Are we Musketeers yet?" Viveca asked, breathless.

"Being a Musketeer is more than fighting," Hélène said. "I can teach you the skills, but only a member of the royal family can appoint you Musketeers." She smiled at them proudly. "No one thinks a girl can be a Musketeer. You must prove them wrong. Meet me here at the same time tomorrow."

With that, Hélène left the room — and the four girls collapsed on the floor, exhausted!

After resting for a few minutes, they returned to the main castle.

"Girls!" Madame de Bossé's voice rang

through the air. The chandelier still hadn't been cleaned up! If Madame saw the mess, they would be in huge trouble.

Corinne ran to the grand entryway and grabbed a feather duster. "Together, we can do this."

In a whirl of cleaning and dusting, the girls used their best Musketeer skills to clean and polish the room until it sparkled. When Madame de Bossé appeared in the doorway, there wasn't a speck of dust to be seen.

The girls fell to the floor the moment she left, giggling in relief.

"Even my eyeballs hurt!" Renée groaned.

Chapter 6

That night, Philippe sat in his study with Brutus the dog at his feet. Bertram, the head guard, stood across from him.

"I don't know what went wrong with the chandelier, my lord!" he said apologetically.

"Accidents do happen. . . ." Philippe began, then pounded his fist on his desk. "But this 'accident' was supposed to finish the prince once and for all! You have failed."

Philippe had been scheming to kill

Prince Louis all along — and Bertram had helped!

"With one small 'accident,' I will take my rightful place on the throne," Philippe went on.

Brutus barked in agreement, and a wicked gleam shone in Philippe's eyes.

"Tomorrow, Louis will be working on his flying contraption in the field," the regent told Bertram. "See to it that he doesn't make it to his coronation."

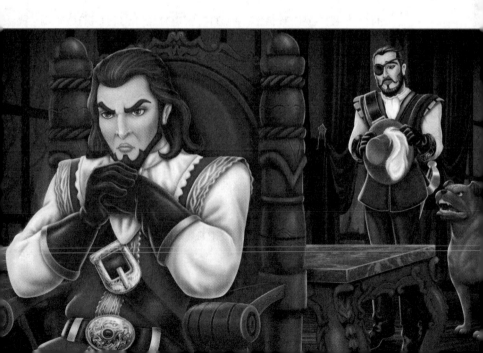

Bertram bowed and turned to leave, calling, "I will not fail you again, Your Highness."

Philippe scowled. "You had better not."

The next morning, Prince Louis stood in an open field behind the castle. He looked up at his half-inflated hot-air balloon, which was tethered to the ground with ropes, and jotted notes in his journal.

"Soon, man will be able to fly!" the prince said to himself.

But the prince didn't see Bertram sneaking around in the shadows, waiting to cut one of the balloon's ropes!

A little while later, the balloon had fully inflated. It floated in the air, held to the ground by a series of ropes. The prince

climbed a ladder to the balloon basket. "Remarkable! I'm truly floating!"

In his excitement, Prince Louis turned up the flame below the balloon, creating more hot air. Bertram darted out and cut one of the remaining ropes holding the balloon to the ground. The balloon strained against its ropes until, one by one, they snapped. The prince was thrown from side to side as each tether broke. He tumbled out of the basket, caught only by a loose rope. . . .

The balloon began to rise through the air, floating across the castle grounds — and taking the prince with it!

"Help!" Prince Louis cried, dangling upside down from the balloon.

On the other side of the castle, Corinne was cleaning dutifully when she heard the prince's calls for help. She leaned out a turret window, just in time to see the prince's balloon approaching. If she didn't act fast, the balloon would hit one of the castle's pointy spires — and pop!

Without hesitating, Corinne grabbed the curtains and used them to swing herself out the window. As the balloon passed, she flipped into the basket. "Hold on!" she called to Prince Louis.

Luckily, the balloon just missed the sharp castle spire, but headed out over the woods. The prince, still dangling from a rope, was about to slam into a giant tree when Corinne turned up the hot air. The balloon rose just in time!

Corinne bent down to pull up Prince Louis's rope. "Are you all right?" she asked, heaving him into the basket.

"I think so," the prince said, shaking a bit.

Corinne held the end of the rope in her hand and couldn't help noticing that it looked like it had been cut — just like the chandelier rope!

Once he got his bearings, the prince introduced himself and thanked Corinne. Now that they were out of danger, they could enjoy the beautiful balloon ride!

"I never thought I'd see Paris from the clouds," Corinne said.

"I always knew I would," Prince Louis replied. "My whole life, it's been my dream to fly." He looked into the sky. "Everyone told me man couldn't fly. But sometimes you have to pursue your dreams . . ."

". . . even when everyone else says it's impossible," Corinne finished. That was exactly what her father used to tell her!

Prince Louis sighed, suddenly sad.

"Once I'm king, there won't be time for my inventions."

Corinne looked him in the eye. "Just because you have your feet firmly on the ground doesn't mean you can't keep reaching for the sky."

Prince Louis smiled, impressed.

Before long, the balloon began to run out of fuel, and Prince Louis steered it back toward the castle field.

"Too bad we can't stay up here forever." Corinne sighed. "It's like anything you wish could come true!"

The prince studied her. "What is your wish, Corinne?"

Corinne hesitated. How would the prince react to her dream? "I want to be a Musketeer," she admitted.

Prince Louis burst out laughing. "But girls can't be Musketeers!"

At that moment, the balloon landed heavily in the field. Corinne and Prince Louis both lurched forward and bumped into each other. Corinne quickly moved away, still stinging from the prince's comment.

"How is it that a prince can envision a man flying in the air, but not a girl as a Musketeer?" she cried, storming off toward the castle.

The regent's guards thundered up to the balloon on horseback, calling out to make sure the prince was all right. But Prince Louis could only watch Corinne go, intrigued by the brave girl who had saved him.

Chapter 7

Back in the castle, Corinne rushed to the training room. She was late! The other girls and Hélène were already practicing. Even Miette was there, with a mini wooden sword on her paw.

"Girls can't be Musketeers. Ha!" said Corinne, still annoyed at Prince Louis. "And after I just saved the prince's life!"

"You saved the prince?" Viveca asked, dropping her sword.

Aramina sighed. "That's so romantic!"

"We could have helped," Renée said, frowning.

Corinne shook her head. "There wasn't time. I was cleaning the turret windows when his balloon went out of control."

"But I thought he was just doing tests," Renée said.

"He was." Corinne nodded. "But the

ropes must have broken . . . or been cut. Just like the chandelier." She pulled the red gem out of her pocket and showed it to the girls. "I found this near the chandelier rope. Maybe it means something."

Hélène studied the gem. "What you are suggesting is very serious. Keep your eyes and ears open. You must be prepared for anything."

The four girls nodded solemnly.

"The prince may be in grave danger," Hélène added quietly.

Corinne and her friends continued their Musketeer training whenever possible. If they couldn't sneak away to the training room, they practiced while doing their chores. They even twirled their brooms like swords as they swept the floors! Before long, the four girls were working together like true Musketeers.

One night, they headed home from the castle with their swords in hand. They'd had a great training session and were playfully jabbing the air and spinning lightly on their toes. Suddenly, a cry for help echoed from the other side of the river.

"Let's go!" Corinne called, running across the bridge.

When they arrived in town, they found that all the vendor carts were abandoned except for one. A man had stayed late to pack up his fruits and vegetables. Now he was surrounded by five frightening robbers — all holding swords!

Desperate, the vendor handed over a small sack of coins. "Today's earnings. Take everything," he said desperately, waving his hand toward the fruits and vegetables.

One mugger grinned and grabbed an apple. "Why, thank you," he snarled. But before he could bite into the apple, it was sliced in two by a whizzing arrow!

"Leave him alone!" Corinne called as the four girls appeared out of the shadows. Renée's bow was loaded with another arrow.

The muggers laughed. "Ooh, we're so scared! Why don't you girlies run along? You don't know who you're dealing with."

"Neither do you," Corinne said bravely.

With that, the girls leaped into action. Corinne flipped up onto a wooden crate. One mugger jabbed the crate with his sword and fell over, surprised. Nearby, Viveca battled another mugger, whipping a wide ribbon from her sleeves and using it to trip him! Aramina and Renée furiously threw fruits and veggies at the men.

Finally, all four girls teamed up to send a tower of wooden crates and sacks of potatoes tumbling down upon the thieves. The men had no choice except to flee — but the lead robber made sure to take the vendor's money with him.

"You're not going anywhere!" Corinne yelled, following him through the streets.

The thief ran up an iron stairwell at the end of an alley, while Corinne flipped and tumbled along the beams outside the stairwell, racing him to the rooftop. She had him cornered! With a single swipe of her sword, she jabbed the bag of coins and flung it up into her hand. "This doesn't belong to you," Corinne said, watching the man run into the darkness.

Back on the ground, Corinne joined her friends and returned the money to the grateful vendor. Triumphant, they headed down the street.

Before long, the girls rounded a corner and came to a stop. One of the regent's wagons was parked in front of a dark warehouse. A group of men loaded wooden crates into the wagon.

The girls ducked out of sight. "What are they doing here?" Aramina wondered.

Bertram stepped out of the shadows and sliced the ropes on one of the crates. As he did, Corinne spotted red gems glistening on the handle of his knife. One of the gems was missing!

She pulled the gem from her pocket. "That's the knife that was used to cut the chandelier!"

Bertram opened the crate and pulled out a jeweled belt. "These are perfect costumes for the prince's masquerade ball," he sneered to one of his men. He pushed a button, revealing a sword on the belt. "The prince won't know what hit him."

The girls gasped.

"The regent's men are planning to sneak weapons into the ball!" Renée whispered.

Corinne jumped to her feet. "To the castle — we've got to warn the prince!"

Chapter 8

Corinne and her friends rushed to the servants' entrance of the castle. By the time they arrived, the wagon they had seen in town was parked outside. Some of the crates had already been unloaded.

Corinne pounded on the door, and Madame de Bossé flung it open unhappily. She wore a nightgown, and her hair was in curlers. "What are you doing here at this hour?"

"We must see the prince!" Corinne said urgently.

"He is in danger!" Aramina added.

Madame rolled her eyes. "The prince has Monsieur Treville and the regent looking after him. He doesn't need help from four meddling girls." She tried to close the door, but Renée stuck her foot in the way. Before Madame de Bossé knew what had happened, the four girls had lifted her up, carried her outside, and hurried into the castle. They slammed the door, leaving Madame de Bossé out in the cold!

Corinne led the way into the ballroom, where Monsieur Treville and Philippe were making sure everything was in place for the masquerade ball. "We must speak to the prince!" she announced.

"The regent and his men are plotting against him!"

Philippe stepped forward. "Is this a joke?" he asked, raising an eyebrow.

"How do you know about this 'plot'?" Monsieur Treville asked the girls. "What proof do you have?"

Corinne's eyes fell on a stack of wooden crates in the corner. They looked just like the crates she'd seen on the regent's wagon!

"Inside those crates are weapons to be used at the ball," she said, pointing.

Renée chimed in. "We heard one of the regent's men talking about it in town."

"This is rubbish!" Philippe scoffed. "My men have all sworn loyalty to the prince."

Monsieur Treville gestured to one of his

men to open a crate. Inside were silly fake sword decorations — not weapons at all!

"They are themed decorations for the prince's Sword Dance at the ball," Philippe explained, picking up a sword and breaking it in half. "They are harmless."

But Corinne knew what she had seen back in town. "There *are* real swords! Open the other crates!"

"Corinne, you must stop this

foolishness," Monsieur Treville said gently.

A group of Musketeers grasped the four girls' arms firmly, leading them out of the castle.

Corinne turned to plead with Monsieur Treville one last time. "You said if I ever needed anything, to come to you."

The leader of the Musketeers shook his head. "I extended you that courtesy because I knew your father. But what would your father say if he saw you now?"

Corinne flinched.

Without another word, she let the Musketeers lead her out of the castle with her friends. Even Miette the kitten was rounded up. As they were all tossed out the door, they could hear Madame de Bossé calling after them, "I never want to see any of you in this castle again — you are all fired!"

The next morning, the four girls began to pack up their apartment. They weren't allowed back in the castle, so they would have to search for jobs elsewhere.

"So much for being Musketeers," Renée said, sighing.

"What are we going to do?" Aramina asked.

Viveca shrugged sadly. "We're all going to go back home and forget about this."

Corinne held her sword in one hand, watching it catch the light. "We shouldn't leave," she said suddenly. "There's still a plot against the prince."

"Everyone thinks we're wrong," Viveca said.

"But *we* know we're right," Corinne countered. "Who knows the castle better than we do? We've cleaned every inch of the place!"

"The guards will be at the doors, looking out for us," Renée said skeptically.

Viveca grinned. "We'll need costumes, so we're not recognized!"

Miette scooped up a stray feather from the ground and batted it over to Corinne. Corinne held it over her face like a mask.

"It's a masquerade ball!" she cried. "No one will recognize us wearing these."

Viveca's eyes lit up, and she began unpacking her fabric and supplies as quickly as she could. "I'll make us the most beautiful gowns and masks!"

"We'll need new weapons that blend in with our costumes," Corinne added.

Renée jumped to her feet. "I'm on it!"

"And I'll teach you all how to dance," Aramina said.

Corinne held out her hand, and one by one, the other girls put their hands on top. Even Miette added a paw! "All for one . . ." Corinne began.

"And one for all!" they chorused.

Chapter 9

Later that evening, Prince Louis said a sad good-bye to the regent. Now that the prince was eighteen, Philippe's job was done, so he was leaving the castle. But Prince Louis didn't know what the regent had up his sleeve. . . .

No sooner had Philippe driven out of sight than people in amazing costumes began arriving at the castle. The masquerade ball was about to begin!

Among the crowd were four lovely girls

wearing elaborate gowns and beautiful masks that hid their faces. Corinne, Viveca, Aramina, and Renée were perfectly disguised! They snuck into the castle using one of the secret passageways and then hurried into the ballroom without being recognized.

Inside, the four girls went separate ways and did their best to blend in, watching everything around them carefully. They would make sure the prince was safe!

Before long, Prince Louis was announced. He entered the ballroom, walking down a grand staircase and taking his place in the center of the dance floor.

"The prince's Sword Dance," the announcer boomed.

Prince Louis looked around the room, surveying many smiling faces before settling on the masked Corinne. He didn't think he had ever seen her before, but there was something about her that intrigued him! "May I have the honor?" he asked, extending his hand.

Surprised and stammering, Corinne accepted (with a nudge from Aramina).

As they spun around the dance floor, Prince Louis looked into Corinne's eyes. "Do I know you?"

"Uh, no, Your Highness," Corinne responded quickly.

Just as the prince was about to ask her another question, the music changed and others joined in the dance.

Among the dancers was a tall man in a lion mask. It was Philippe, moving ever closer to the prince. While everyone else did the Sword Dance with fake swords, Philippe's sword was real. He had snuck it

in on his belt, just as the girls had feared! It gleamed in the ballroom lights, catching Renée's eye.

Renée gestured frantically to Corinne, who spun the prince out of Philippe's reach. Aramina gracefully danced over to the regent, cutting in, and then stepped on his toes every time he inched closer to the prince.

"Sorry, I'm not much of a dancer," Aramina said sweetly.

As the dance went on, everyone moved the ceremonial swords closer and closer to the prince. Fireworks boomed outside the castle windows, and the crowd gasped in excitement. While they were distracted, Philippe lunged for the prince — with his real sword!

Corinne grabbed Philippe's wrist,

wrestling the sword from his hand before anyone noticed. But then *she* was the one holding the real sword, pointed right at the prince.

"Her sword is real!" Philippe cried. "Someone stop her!"

The regent's men pulled the prince out of the ballroom in a flash. The Musketeers were nowhere to be seen, thanks to Philippe's scheming.

"The real villain is getting away!" Corinne cried as Philippe's guards surrounded them.

Renée, Viveca, and Aramina rushed to her side. "And those men are all in on it!" Renée added.

"We're not going to let them get away with this," Corinne said determinedly.

In the blink of an eye, the girls' costumes

were transformed into capes, skirts, leggings, and boots. Swords and weapons were unsheathed, and the four friends suddenly looked like fierce Musketeers! They each struck a fighting pose and turned to face the regent's men.

The fight was on — and the prince's life depended on the outcome!

Chapter 10

Philippe led Prince Louis from the ballroom and into a secret passageway. Corinne and her friends knew he was up to no good, but before they could follow him, they had to get past his men!

Luckily, Hélène had trained the girls well. Corinne held her own fighting against three of the regent's guards at once. She flipped and dodged out of the way with ease, while Viveca tied up two others

with ribbons flung from her sleeves. Aramina whipped her wrists and threw fans like boomerangs around the room. Even Hélène got in on the action, innocently tripping one of the henchmen and knocking into another with the handle of her broom.

Renée used her slingshot necklace to

fling gems at some of the henchmen across the room. When she noticed that Corinne was in trouble, she borrowed a violin and bow from a nearby musician. She shot the bow across the room, cutting a cord, which dropped a big banner on Corinne's opponent's head. "E-string's a little flat," said Renée with a smile.

Before the girls could get their bearings, another group of the regent's men swarmed into the ballroom. Corinne and her friends were cornered, still fighting hard.

"Where's the prince?" Corinne called to the others.

Renée blocked a shot from one of the men. "I thought you were watching him!"

"I got a little distracted!" Corinne replied, glancing frantically around the room. She noticed that one of the wall panels in the back was cracked open. "The passageways!"

With a spray of her glitter perfume bottle, Viveca created a distraction. The four girls bolted to the passageway, with the regent's henchmen on their heels. They toppled a bookcase behind them, blocking the men for a moment.

With Corinne in the lead, the girls rounded a corner and came across Monsieur Treville and his Musketeers. They had been tied up!

As her friends unknotted the ropes, Corinne continued down the passage in search of the prince. Through a peephole, she could see Philippe and Prince Louis climbing a nearby stairwell. She raced up a parallel set of stairs, all the way to the roof.

Philippe led Prince Louis to the castle rooftop, assuring him that he was just trying to keep him safe. But Prince Louis was suspicious. "This is a dead end," he said, peering around the roof.

Philippe smiled wickedly. "That's right, cousin. A dead . . . end." In one movement, he flicked the bejeweled sword from his belt and swiped at the prince! "All

these years I advised you, to be tossed out the day you become king."

The prince dodged Philippe's sword. "I didn't choose to be king!"

"I should be king, not you!" Philippe spat.

Just then, Corinne reached the top of her staircase, on the other side of the roof. A big gap separated her from Philippe and the prince. From where she stood, it was clear that Philippe was about to hurt the prince. She had to act fast!

With a flying leap, Corinne grabbed a banner hanging from one of the castle turrets. She used it to swing across the gap, flipping through the air and landing on her feet — right between Philippe and Prince Louis.

"You will never be king!" she told Philippe, raising her sword.

Corinne and the regent fought hard, their swords clinking and clanging in the moonlight. But with one powerful swipe, Philippe knocked the weapon out of Corinne's hand. He raised his sword threateningly at Corinne and Prince Louis.

"Your persistence is quite useful," he said to Corinne, smirking. "I can tell everyone that when you couldn't finish off the prince at the ball, you came up here for one final battle." He chuckled, pleased with his story. "I'll say that I was too late to help the prince. And when you lunged at me, I had no choice but to send you off the roof."

While Philippe was distracted, the prince reached out his foot and kicked

Corinne's sword over to her. She grabbed it, flipped to her feet, and began to battle Philippe once again.

"Nice story," she told the regent. "Too bad yours won't have a happy ending!"

This time, Corinne and Prince Louis teamed up against Philippe. Despite his best efforts, they soon defeated him. As

Corinne pointed her sword at Philippe, Monsieur Treville bolted out onto the roof, followed by his Musketeers, as well as by Viveca, Aramina, and Renée.

The Musketeers wasted no time in arresting the regent, while the girls rushed up to Corinne. "You did it!" Aramina cried.

Corinne smiled at her friends. "No, *we* did it," she said.

Out in front of the castle, Philippe was loaded into a wagon with Bertram and his other henchmen. Philippe begged the prince to let him explain, but Prince Louis wasn't interested in hearing any more lies. He sent the wagon away.

Corinne, Viveca, Aramina, and Renée stood nearby, still wearing their costumes and masks. Prince Louis approached them.

"I want to see the faces of my rescuers," he said.

Slowly, each girl removed her mask. The prince looked especially delighted to recognize Corinne. But before he could say anything, Madame de Bossé interrupted. "Your Highness, those girls have been banned from the castle!"

Prince Louis looked at Corinne. "Is this true?"

Corinne nodded, lowering her eyes.

Prince Louis thought for a moment. "After what you've done, you girls don't belong at the castle."

Was he going to kick them out again?

Chapter 11

"Your place is with the Musketeers," Prince Louis said. He never intended to ban Corinne and her friends from the castle.

The prince was crowned and became the king of France. The next day, the new king's first order of business was to make all four girls official Musketeers!

King Louis stood before a crowd gathered outside of the castle. "My first decree as king is to recognize the courage of those who fought to ensure that this day would come to be." He called Corinne, Viveca, Aramina, and Renée to his side. "You have committed the highest act of courage and nobility. I hereby anoint you, now and forever, as Musketeers!"

Confetti rained down from a hot-air balloon, and the crowd cheered wildly. Hélène watched the girls with pride, Corinne's mother stood nearby, her eyes sparkling with happy tears, and even Miette

was made an honorary Mus-cat-eer! After the ceremony, the girls made their way through the crowd, wearing their new Musketeer hats and capes. They smiled and waved at Hélène. The new king had put her in charge, and she was enjoying bossing around Madame de Bossé!

Corinne's mother rushed over and wrapped her daughter in a hug. "My little girl's a Musketeer!" she cried. "I knew you could do it."

Corinne smiled widely. "Thanks for believing in me, Mom."

King Louis approached the girls. "How are my favorite Musketeers doing?" he asked.

Corinne couldn't pass up an opportunity to tease him. "I thought you didn't believe that girls could be Musketeers."

King Louis smiled sheepishly. "If a man can fly, surely a girl can be a Musketeer, right?" he said, looking around at the girls.

Then King Louis turned to Corinne. "I was thinking perhaps, to celebrate, you might, um, want to take another balloon ride with me?" he asked hopefully.

But before Corinne could answer, Monsieur Treville rode up on horseback. "We have just received word of a plot against the king!" he called.

Corinne smiled at the king's invitation, then told him, "We'll have to take the balloon ride later," she said, whistling to Alexander and leaping easily into his saddle.

Grinning, Corinne and her friends were ready for their first task as official Musketeers!

"All for one, and one for all!" the four girls called, riding into the sunset. Another adventure awaited them!

ALL-NEW *Barbie*™ MOVIE
ON DVD FALL 2009!

Add these great DVDs to your collection!